THE HOUSE

Carol Watson
Illustrated by Colin King

Series Editor: Heather Amery
Consultant: Betty Root

It has

a very tall chimney,  a bright red roof,

five windows and a big green door.

In the kitchen

The dog chases the cat

across the sink,

under the cooker,

over the table

and round the bin.

They knock down

cups and saucers,

a big saucepan,

a plate of cakes

and the red apron.

The men have come to paint the living room.

We take down

the three pictures,

the orange curtains,

the old mirror

and the dusty clock.

They carry out

the small table, a big chair,

the television and the rug.

The men have finished.

Dad keeps his car in the garage.

We help him to

wash the bonnet,

polish the lights,

clean the windscreen and the wheels.

In the garden Dad likes to

dig the ground,

plant the seeds,

water the flowers

and sweep up the leaves.

We play in the garden.

We chase butterflies, pick up worms,

hide in the bushes and climb the trees.

17

It is bathtime.

In the bath

we turn on the taps,

splash the water,

make some bubbles

and play with the soap.

Bedtime

At bedtime

we take off our shoes

and socks,

look for a hairbrush

and find a comb.

Dad puts us to bed.   He reads a book to us,

draws the curtains and kisses us goodnight.

Here is a puzzle.

Can you find mum, dad, baby, the cat, two worms and a spotty dog?

First published in 1980
by Usborne Publishing Ltd
20 Garrick Street
London WC2 9BJ, England
© Usborne Publishing Ltd 1980

Printed in Belgium

The name Usborne and the device are Trade Marks of Usborne Publishing Ltd.

All rights reserved. No part of this publication may be reproduced, stored in a retrieval system or transmitted in any form or by any means, electronic, mechanical, photocopying, recording or otherwise, without the prior permission of the publisher.